Q READS

BLOOD AND BASKETBALL

JANICE GREENE

SADDLEBACK
EDUCATIONAL PUBLISHING

▊QREADS

SADDLEBACK
EDUCATIONAL PUBLISHING
www.sdlback.com

ISBN-13: 978-1-61651-213-2
ISBN-10: 1-61651-213-X
eBook: 978-1-60291-935-8

Printed in the U.S.A.
20 19 18 17 16   6 7 8 9 10

■ ■ ■

Carl, the owner of the Jackson Eagles, punched a button on the remote control. "Just look at this," he said.

Ed, the coach, turned to watch. On the screen, a player with floppy blond hair twisted away from a guard and scored. His moves were amazingly quick.

"Yeah, Dale Curtis," Ed said. "I've seen him. I don't want him."

"Come on, man!" Carl said. "He could be the next Larry Bird!"

"He's a problem waiting to happen," Ed said. "The kid is only 18, just out of high school. And he's on his own—no family. The word is he's been living with a neighbor or something."

"But the *team*'s like a family," Carl went on. "Once he's on the team—"

"Once he's on the team, he's an instant millionaire," Ed interrupted. "He's instantly famous. It's too much for most kids. Remember Reed Stevenson?"

Carl frowned. At first, young Stevenson had been a great player. Then he'd discovered gambling and drugs. It had been an ugly year-and-a-half for the Mississippi team.

"I'm not cleaning up after another kid like that," Ed insisted.

Carl stared at the screen. Dale spun through the key and left the floor effortlessly. He seemed to float toward the basket. Below him, a guard's mouth dropped open. The ball swished through the net, sweet and clean.

"Maybe Will Bishop would take him on as a roommate," Carl suggested. "Bishop had it tough growing up, too. But he's a real steady guy. He could be like an older brother."

Ed disagreed. "Dale's older brother, Bode, is the only family the kid has. And Bode can't time later, he came home exhausted and fell asleep in minutes. If his mother was still crying, he didn't hear her.

■ ■ ■

Dale peered out Will's front window. Still no Bode. He should have arrived hours ago.

Dale couldn't wait to move to his own place. Will had rules—a lot of them. Yet Will himself was generous and smart. He told Dale a lot about his teammates and how they played. And he seemed to know everything about the rival teams.

Dale was at the window again when a rental car pulled into the driveway. "Bode!" he yelled. He ran outside just as his brother opened the car door.

For a moment, the brothers just stared at each other. Bode was six-eight, an inch shorter and 40 pounds heavier than Dale. His arms were covered with tattoos. A thick scar encircled his wrist like a bracelet.

Dale smelled alcohol when he hugged

Bode. "Get on in here!" he said to his brother. "You hungry? Got lots of stuff to eat here!"

"Nah," Bode said, as they walked inside. "I just want to be out of that car for a while."

"I'm gonna get you a car!" Dale said excitedly. "Something real cool—with leather and everything."

"That'd be real nice, Dale," he said as he grinned at his brother. "Look at you—a *rich* guy! It's like a dream, huh?"

"As long as I don't wake up, it's okay with me," Dale agreed.

"Fine-looking place," Bode said as he looked around the large living room. "That TV is as big as a fireplace! There's nothing like that in the hole. We didn't even get cable."

Dale punched the remote until he found a basketball game. The New Jersey Nets were playing the Miami Heat. "I'll get you a TV, too," he said, "even bigger than this."

Bode smiled. "You got a good heart, kid. Not like most people. But now that you've got money—watch out. People you've never even heard of, so-called friends—they'll another man intercepted. He took a shot at Nikki's glass. Jumping back to catch it, Nikki slammed into a man behind her.

The man grabbed Nikki's glass, spilling half her drink. By now, a large circle of people, laughing and shouting, were in on the game.

The party got crazier as the night went on. Bode filled Dale's glass again and again. It was so crowded he kept stepping on people's feet. Nikki fell on a lamp and broke it. When Cici told her to leave, Nikki started shouting and Cici yelled back.

Dale fell asleep on the way home. He'd tried to remember to set the alarm clock before going to bed. But it was nine o'clock when he woke up. He was late for practice. An hour late.

Dressing in a panic, he felt dizzy and sick. He raced to the practice gym and walked in slowly, hoping no one would notice. Rick snickered when he saw him. Then Will came up and said, "Coach wants you in his office."

Ed was hunched over his computer. He glanced at Dale, then turned back to the screen. "You're suspended," he snapped. "Come back in three days." His voice was distant and cold.

Dale waited for him to say more, but the coach's eyes stayed glued to the computer screen.

Dale threw up on the way back to his car. Later, after practice, Will said, "Maybe we should start placing bets, Dale. Think you can last another week on the team?"

Dale was too miserable to answer.

Bode was outraged when he heard that Dale had been suspended. "They act like you're just some kid off the street," he said. "Just a nobody!"

Dale said, "I *am* just a nobody until I start helping the team."

"No, you're the *star*!" Bode said. "You're better than any of them."

Dale grinned. Bode had always been good at making him feel better.

■ ■ ■

Three days later, Dale was back on the practice court. Three days after that, the Eagles left for New York. Their first game of the season was against the New York City Hawks.

Dale found himself matched up with Burnell Simms, one of the quickest guys in the NBA.

Two minutes into the game, Dale was guarding Simms. The net was clear. Dale moved to block him—too late! The ball swished through the basket and the crowd whooped.

Simms stole the ball from Dale twice. Again and again, he was able to slip away from Dale and score. But the rookie was learning. Dale was getting better at spotting him. By halftime, though, the Hawks led, 50 to 22.

In the locker room Dale was pacing, full of nervous energy. Will came up to him and said, "You're gaining on him."

Dale smiled. "Yeah, but I haven't quite got him yet," he answered.

"Don't worry, you will," Will said in a confident voice.

Dale sat down and turned a ball slowly in his hands. His breath became calm and slow. *Yeah, I'm gonna catch him*, he whispered to himself.

Next time Dale had the ball, Simms lunged for it. Just as Simms' fingers brushed the ball, Dale swerved away and took his shot. The ball missed, but Will was under it. Leaping back, he passed the ball to Dale. This time he sprang away from Simms' grasping hands and put the ball through the hoop. Nothing but net.

"All *right!*" Will yelled.

Dale made another basket, and another. With two seconds left to go, the ball was in his hands again. From 30 feet out, he made a basket. The Eagles won, 67 to 58. Dale had scored 21 points—more than any other player.

Inside the locker room, everyone crowded around Dale. "You beat Simms!" Will shouted.

"You beat him!" As players slapped Dale's back, Rick yelled, "The ceiling! Take this man to the ceiling!"

"Lie down!" Tyrone commanded. Glancing around nervously, Dale obeyed. Smiling, sweaty faces were all around him. Then, slowly, he was hoisted up by a dozen strong hands. Up, up . . . "Touch the ceiling!" Rick cried out.

As Dale reached up and touched the ceiling, the players roared. "You did it!" Will yelled. "You're the *man!*" hollered Tyrone.

Dale had never been so happy in his life. He was on top of the world.

Visitors started to crowd into the locker room. For a few moments, Dale was alone. Bode was back in Jackson, shopping for his new car. Then some of Dale's teammates introduced him to their wives and girlfriends, brothers and sisters, mothers and fathers. Then Will cut through the crowd. A strong-looking, white-haired woman was holding onto his arm.

"Dale," he said proudly, "I'd like you to

meet my mom."

Dale shook her hand. It felt as tough as his shoes. Her eyes were bright and piercing. Dale had the feeling that she'd been through a lot.

"Will tells me that you have a lot of promise," she said.

A lot of promise, Dale thought. *I could make it. Or I could lose it all.*

On the plane back to Jackson, Will sat by Dale. "Mom wants you to come to the house and visit sometime."

"I'd like that," Dale smiled. "She's something, your mom."

"Thanks. You're sure right about that," Will agreed. "What happened to *your* mom, anyway?"

Dale hesitated. He never talked about his mom's death—not even to Bode. But now the words poured out of him. "She was walking home after working the late shift. Some guy drove right into her on a crosswalk. He took off and they never caught him. I wish *I'd* caught him."

"It wouldn't have brought her back," Will said softly.

Dale let that sink in.

Then Will added, "Basketball helps somehow, doesn't it?"

Dale nodded. "Yeah," he said. "For some reason it does."

■ ■ ■

It was two days before the game with the Houston Rockets. About 10:00 P.M., Bode drove up to Will's house in his new car. It was a white Cadillac Escalade. Bode had added all the extras, including special rims and a state-of-the-art sound system.

"Come on!" Bode urged his brother. "We gotta take this baby out!"

Dale had been playing a video game with Will. "I don't know, Bode," he said. "We've got a big practice early tomorrow morning."

"We're not going to be out all night or nothing," Bode insisted. "Just take a break and have a little fun."

"Wouldn't be smart to make it a late

night," Will said.

"I'm talking to my brother. Don't you butt in, man!" Bode snapped.

Embarrassed, Dale put his hand on Bode's arm. "Bode, take it easy," he said softly.

"You're his brother," Will went on, "but you're not looking out for him!"

The veins in Bode's neck popped out as he shouted, "Don't ever say that, man! Nobody ever looked out for my brother like I did! *Nobody!*"

"If he sticks with you, he's gonna get kicked off the team!" Will warned.

Bode was furious. His hand shot toward his pocket.

Will stepped back. "Don't you even *think* about pulling your knife on me, or I'm calling the cops!" he shouted.

Bode got right in Will's face and sneered. "I got you scared, huh!"

"Get out of my house, you loser!" Will said. "*Now!*"

"What'd you call me?" Bode yelled.

Dale gripped Bode's arm. "Let it go!" he

begged. "Come on!"

Bode headed for the door. "You coming with me, then?" he asked.

Dale got up. "Yeah," he said. He didn't look back at Will.

In the car, Bode turned to Dale. "First thing tomorrow, I'm looking for a place for the two of us," he said.

"Okay. Sounds good," said Dale.

■ ■ ■

Fifteen minutes later, they were speeding up a long hill toward the Diamond Valley Golf Club. A kid about 15 sat in the back seat. The boy, Gibb, had lived next door to them in the old neighborhood. Bode had picked him up when he saw him hitchhiking.

Twice, Dale had glanced in the rearview mirror and seen Will's car following them. He didn't mention it.

Piled in the trunk area were two golf bags, stuffed full of clubs. They looked brand new. Dale wondered if Bode was planning to play golf. It was dark outside—and neither of them knew how to play! But that wouldn't matter to Bode.

Bode was on his cell phone. He'd made about 10 calls since they'd left Will's house. "The parking lot. At 10:30," he'd told everyone.

Several cars were already there when they pulled into the lot. Bode took a long drink from a bottle he'd had in his pocket. His eyes glittered. He held out the bottle to Dale, but Dale shook his head. Everyone gathered around to admire the new Escalade.

More cars and trucks pulled up. Thumping music and loud shouts filled the cold night air.

Bode got up on the hood of a truck. "Let's play some golf!" he shouted.

"Ha! Golf's for rich people!" yelled a woman in the crowd.

"Yeah? Well, *we're* rich!" Bode shouted. "We're stinking rich!" He hopped down and sauntered to the back of the Escalade.

He yanked open the door and threw the golf bags out of the car. The shiny clubs tumbled out onto the pavement.

With whoops and yells, everyone ran to grab a club. Two women tugged at each end of the same putter.

Bode held up a golf ball. "All right!" he yelled. *"Go get it!"* Then, with a mighty heave, he threw the ball far out on the fairway.

The crowd started to run, yelling and swinging their clubs.

Bode laughed as he got back in the car. "Come on!" he cried out. Dale and Gibb quickly scrambled in after him.

Dale was nervous. "Bode, I don't know about this," he said.

Bode gunned the motor. "Relax, kid," he said in a slurred voice. "Nobody's gonna get hurt."

The Escalade roared across the golf course. When the crowd realized what Bode was doing, they turned around and ran toward their cars.

Bode raced across the dark grass toward the ball. With one hand on the steering wheel, he leaned out the window and swung his club. The head of the club missed the ball by inches.

Bode made a tight turn. A red pickup streaked across the grass, just to the left of the ball. Bode swerved in front of it. The truck came so close, Dale could see the driver's frightened face.

Again, Bode leaned out the window. This time, with a loud *whack!* the ball flew toward the trees at the far edge of the grass, bouncing in the headlights.

Again, Bode zoomed after the ball. Engines roared behind him. Suddenly, a man came running out from the trees, waving his arms.

"It's Will!" Dale said. "*Stop*, Bode!"

The Escalade plowed to a stop, spraying soft dirt onto Will's legs.

"Get out of the way, or get under my wheels!" Bode shrieked.

Will didn't move.

Dale got out and ran up to him. Bode got out, too, yelling, "You're gonna get it now, man!"

Then two things happened at once. Gibb

scrambled into the Escalade's driver's seat and took off. And three police cars, with their sirens wailing, pulled into the parking lot.

"*Dale, come on!*" Will cried out. He started jogging toward the trees. Bode stood still, watching as Gibb sped across the grass in the new Escalade.

"*Bode!*" Dale grabbed his arm.

They ran. Will led them through the trees to where his car was parked on the other side of the golf course.

Dale looked back as they drove away. The patrol cars' searchlights revealed rows of ugly ruts where tire tracks crisscrossed the grass.

■ ■ ■

The game with the Rockets was at the Jackson Dome. Dale drove, and Bode came with him.

They pulled into the VIP section of the parking lot. Bode said, "Let's go in to see if anyone famous is here yet."

"Nah, I don't feel like it," Dale said in an unusually serious voice. Bode looked at him in surprise.

"That kid, Gibb . . ." Dale went on. "You told the cops he stole your car."

"I *had* to," Bode said. "If they'd found out I was trespassing on that golf course—I'd be back in prison, just like that! And I'm not going back."

"But now Gibb is locked up in juvenile detention," Dale said.

"Kid, I would have gone to a *real prison*," Bode said angrily. "Juvenile detention's nothing like that. Besides, that kid got *himself* in trouble. He didn't have to take my car. He didn't have to come with me, for that matter."

"I shouldn't have come, either," Dale said in a soft, sad, low voice.

Bode was disgusted. "Oh, *man*! You know what you sound like?" he growled. "You sound just like that goody-goody mama's boy *Will*."

Dale's voice was a warning. "Will's my friend," he said.

"Yeah? But he's not *family*. He's not *blood*," Bode reminded him. "Look—whose side are you on?"

"*Mine*," said Dale. "That's why I'm sticking with Will. I'll see you around, Bode. But I'm through doing crazy stuff with you. No more, man."

Bode's hand balled into a tight fist and slammed down hard on the dashboard. "You'll see me *around*?" he asked in astonishment. "Like you expect me to make an appointment with you or something? Is this what I get after looking out for you all those years? You get rich and famous and then you just push me out!"

"You can't stay out of trouble, Bode!" Dale cried out. "I'm not going to let you take me down with you!"

Bode shoved Dale so hard his head banged against the window. Then, swearing, Bode opened the door and got out. "That's it, man!" he said. "Just forget about me—'cause I'm out of your life for good. You're nothing to me, man! *Nothing!*"

And he walked away.

Dale rubbed his head for a minute. Then

he walked into the dome and went to find a quiet corner in the locker room.

A few minutes later, he heard the sound of a ball bouncing behind him.

Will sat down next to him and handed Dale the ball. Pretending not to notice Dale's tears, he said, "You ready to go out and win us a game?"

Slowly, Dale smiled. "Yeah," he said.

Dale Curtis made 38 points that night. The Eagles won, 104 to 98.

■ ■ ■

Dale celebrated the holidays with Will's family that year. A month later he started dating Sue, one of Will's cousins. He also started taking some community college courses on the Internet. His game got better and better. At the end of the season, he was named Rookie of the Year.

Several weeks after the game with the Rockets, Bode had been sent back to prison for selling drugs. Dale wrote to him, but Bode never answered.

After-Reading Wrap-Up

1. Do you like the title of this book? Why or why not? Use your imagination to help you come up with two alternative titles.

2. Which character in *Blood and Basketball* was most like you? Which one was least like you? Explain your answers.

3. Most of the sad and difficult things in Dale's young life had been out of his control. As the story progressed, a very important decision was *in* his control. Do you think he chose wisely? Give two reasons to support your opinion.

4. Do you think team owners and coaches often disagree about a player's value to the team? Who do you suppose usually wins the argument? Why?

5. Should top college athletes be required to graduate before being eligible to play in the pros? List two arguments *for* that requirement and two arguments *against* it.

6. What character in the story had the most positive influence on Dale's life? List three contributions that character made to Dale's eventual success.